Published in the United States of America by Star Bright Books, Inc. The name Star Bright Books and the Star Bright Books logo are registered trademarks of Star Bright Books, Inc. Please visit www.starbrightbooks.com. For bulk orders, contact: orders@ starbrightbooks.com, or call customer service at: (718) 784-9112.

Hardback ISBN-13: 978-1-59572-345-1
Paperback ISBN-13: 978-1-59572-346-8

Star Bright Books / NY / 00111110
Printed in China (WKT) 10 9 8 7 6 5 4 3 2 1

Library of Congress Cataloging-in-Publication Data

Wildsmith, Brian.
 The Bremen town musicians / Brian Wildsmith.
   p. cm.
 Summary: While on their way to Bremen, four aging animals who are no longer of any use to their masters find a new home after outwitting a gang of robbers.
  ISBN 978-1-59572-345-1 (hardcover) -- ISBN 978-1-59572-346-8 (pbk.)
 [1. Fairy tales. 2. Folklore--Germany.] I. Title.
 PZ8.W648Br 2012
 398.2--dc23
 [E]
                        2011032407

THE BREMEN TOWN MUSICIANS

Retold and Illustrated by Brian Wildsmith

Star Bright Books
New York

There was once a farmer who had a donkey
that had worked for him for many years. The
donkey grew old and could not work any more,
so the farmer thought about selling him.

"It's time for me to leave," said the donkey.
"I still have a fine voice. I will go to the famous
city of Bremen and sing with the town band."
And he set off along the highway.

He had not gone very far when he met a dog, lying in the road, and panting as if he were very tired.

"What is the matter?" asked the donkey.

"Ah," said the dog, "I have grown old and weak, and my master thinks about getting rid of me. Now I have run away. But where shall I go? And what shall I do?"

"Come with me," said the donkey. "I am on my way to Bremen. You can bark and I can bray, and together we can sing in the town band."

And so they went along the highway happily together.

After they had travelled a
short distance, they met a cat,
who was looking very sad.

"What is wrong?" asked the
donkey.

"Ah," said the cat, "I can't
catch mice any more and my
mistress says that I am useless.
So I decided to run away. But
what will happen to me now?"

"Come with us to
Bremen," said the donkey.
"You can meow, the dog
can bark, I can bray, and
together we can sing in
the town band."

And so all three
went cheerfully along
the highway.

Not long afterward they came upon a rooster, perched upon a gate, and crowing with all his might.

"Why do you crow so loudly?" asked the donkey.

"The farmer's wife says I am too old to be useful any more," said the rooster. "So I am making as much noise as I can before she puts me in the cooking-pot."

"Why don't you come to Bremen with us?" asked the donkey. "You can crow, the cat can meow, the dog can bark, I can bray, and together we can sing in the town band."

And so all four went along the highway, singing together.

However, time was getting on and the four friends knew they couldn't get to Bremen that day. When night fell, they came to a forest and decided to sleep there.

The donkey and the dog settled down under a tall tree,
while the cat climbed up into the branches.

The rooster flew up to the top of the tree and looked around. In the distance he saw a spark of light.

"Friends,'" he said, "I think there's a house nearby. Let's go and see if we can find some food."

The animals all agreed, so off they went together. Soon they
came upon a house with a bright light streaming from the windows.

The donkey went up to the house and peeped in through a window.

"What do you see in there?" asked the rooster.

"What do I see!" exclaimed the donkey. I see a table full of good things to eat and five fierce robbers standing around it."

"I'd love some of that food," said the dog.
"So would I," said the rooster. "But how do we get in?"

At last the cat thought of a plan. The donkey put his front legs on the windowsill, the dog climbed onto his back, the cat climbed onto the dog, and the rooster flew up and perched on the cat.

"Now!" said the rooster. "Let us all sing together!"

The donkey *brayed*, the dog *barked*, the cat *meowed*, and the rooster *cock-a-doodle-doo-ed*.

Then they all broke through the window at once and tumbled into the room with a terrible noise.

The robbers were so frightened
that they ran out of the house as fast
as their legs would carry them.

The four friends burst out laughing and dove in to
the food on the table. When they had eaten everything in
sight, they settled down and went to sleep.

Meanwhile, one of the robbers crept back inside the house. It was so dark that he stepped on the cat who spat at him, he tripped over the dog who bit him, he bumped into the donkey who kicked him, and then the rooster flew on top of him, crowing away.

The robber was terrified and
ran back to the others. "A terrible old
witch spat at me, a fierce man stabbed
me, a huge monster kicked me, and a
demon screamed in my ear."

At this, the robbers all ran away
and were never seen again.

The friends were all so pleased with the house
that they stayed there and lived happily ever after. And
they never did go and sing in the Bremen Town Band.